"To Mrs. Rubino and her amazing students. Love & Peace. A Pérez 3·17·09

My Very Own Room

Mi propio cuartito

Story by / Escrito por
Amada Irma Pérez

Illustrations by / Ilustrado por
Maya Christina Gonzalez

Children's Book Press / Libros para niños
San Francisco, California

D0516611

Una mañana me desperté en una cama muy apretujada en un cuarto bien lleno. El codo de Víctor me picaba las costillas. Mario había gateado de su cuna hasta nuestra cama. Ahora una pierna suya me cubría la cara y apenas yo podía respirar. Mis otros tres hermanos dormían en la cama juntito a la nuestra.

Yo estaba demasiado grande para esto. Ya iba a cumplir nueve años y estaba cansada de compartir mi cuarto con mis cinco hermanitos. Lo que más deseaba en el mundo era tener mi propio cuartito.

I woke up one morning on a crowded bed in a crowded room. Víctor's elbow was jabbing me in the ribs. Mario had climbed out of his crib and crawled in with us. Now his leg lay across my face and I could hardly breathe. In the bed next to ours my three other brothers were sleeping.

I was getting too big for this. I was almost nine years old, and I was tired of sharing a room with my five little brothers. More than anything in the whole world I wanted a room of my own.

little space was all I wanted, but there wasn't much of it. Our tiny house was shared by eight of us, and sometimes more when our friends and relatives came from Mexico and stayed with us until they found jobs and places to live.

Once a family with eight kids (mostly boys!) lived with us for two months. It was noisy and a lot of fun. There was always a long line to use the bathroom, but the toilet seat was always warm.

Lo único que yo quería era un pequeño espacio, pero eso era lo que no había. Nuestra pequeña casa la compartíamos los ocho miembros de nuestra familia y a veces más, cuando amigos y familiares venían de México y se quedaban con nosotros hasta que hallaban trabajo y un lugar donde vivir.

Una vez una familia con ocho niños (casi puros hombrecitos) vivió con nosotros por dos meses. Había mucho ruido pero era muy divertido. Siempre había una larga fila para usar el excusado, pero el asiento estaba siempre calientito.

5

Sometimes very early in the morning while everyone was still sleeping, I would climb up the crooked ladder that leaned against the elm tree in our backyard. I would sit on a little board, pretending it was a bench, and just think. I could hear my father snoring. He worked all night at the factory and went to bed just before dawn.

I loved my brothers. It wasn't that I didn't want to be near them, I just needed a place of my own.

A veces muy de mañanita mientras todos dormían, me subía por la escalera chueca al olmo del patio de atrás. Me sentaba en una tablita que imaginaba ser una banca y me ponía a pensar. Podía oír a mi papá roncando. Él trabajaba de noche en la fábrica y se iba a dormir un poco antes del amanecer.

Yo amaba a mis hermanos. No era que no quisiera estar junto a ellos, lo único que necesitaba era un lugar mío.

Caminé de puntitas por nuestra casita de dos recámaras. Me asomé detrás de la cortina que mi mamá había hecho con saquitos de harina para separar nuestra sala del cuartito donde guardábamos cosas.

—¡Ajá! ¡Aquí está! Éste puede ser mi cuarto—. Me lo imaginé con mi propia cama, mesa y lámpara, un lugar donde pudiera leer los libros que tanto amaba, escribir en mi diario y soñar.

I tiptoed around our tiny, two bedroom house. I peeked behind the curtain my mother had made from flour sacks to separate our living room from the storage closet.

"Aha! This is it! This could be my room." I imagined it with my own bed, table, and lamp—a place where I could read the books I loved, write in my diary, and dream.

Me senté entre las cajas. Mi mamá debe haberme oído porque ella se acercó desde la cocina.

—Mamá, es perfecto— dije y le conté mi idea.

—Ay, mijita, tú no entiendes. Estamos guardando la máquina de coser de mi hermana y la herramienta para jardín de tu tío. Algún día necesitarán sus cosas para poder vivir mejor aquí en este nuevo país. Y también hay muebles y ropa vieja— dijo, moviendo la cabeza de un lado a otro lentamente.

I sat down among the boxes. My mother must have heard me because she came in from the kitchen.

"Mamá, it's perfect," I said, and I told her my idea.

"Ay, *mijita*, you do not understand. We are storing my sister's sewing machine and your uncle's garden tools. Someday they will need their things to make a better living in this new country. And there's the furniture and old clothes," she said. Slowly she shook her head.

Then she saw the determination on my face and the tears forming in my eyes. "Wait," she said, seriously thinking. "Maybe we could put these things on the back porch and cover them with old blankets."

"And we could put a tarp on top so nothing would get ruined," I added.

"Yes, I think we can do it. Let's take everything out and see how much space there is."

I gave her a great big hug and she kissed me.

Se fijó en la determinación en mi cara y las lágrimas que ya comenzaban a formarse en mis ojos. —Espera— dijo pensando seriamente—. Quizás podamos poner estas cosas en el porche de atrás y cubrirlas con cobijas viejas.

—Y podemos poner una lona para que no se echen a perder— agregué.

—Sí, yo creo que sí podemos hacerlo. Vamos a sacar todo y ver qué tanto espacio tenemos.

Le di un fuerte abrazo y ella me dio un besito.

Después del desayuno, comenzamos a empujar los viejos muebles hacia el porche. Todos ayudaron. Parecíamos un ejército de poderosas hormigas.

Acarreamos muebles, herramienta y máquinas. Arrastramos bolsas bien repletas de ropa vieja y juguetes. Jalamos cajas con tesoros y demasiadas cosas viejas. Finalmente todo estaba fuera excepto algunos botes de pintura que había sobrado de la vez que pintamos la casa.

After breakfast we started pushing the old furniture out to the back porch. Everyone helped. We were like a mighty team of powerful ants.

We carried furniture, tools, and machines. We dragged bulging bags of old clothes and toys. We pulled boxes of treasures and overflowing junk. Finally, everything was out except for a few cans of leftover paint from the one time we had painted the house.

$\mathcal{E}$ach can had just a tiny bit of paint inside. There was pink and blue and white, but not nearly enough of any one color to paint the room.

"I have an idea," I said to my brothers. "Let's mix them!" Héctor and Sergio helped me pour one can into another and we watched the colors swirl together. A new color began to appear, a little like purple and much stronger than pink. Magenta!

We painted and painted until we ran out of paint.

$\mathcal{C}$ada bote contenía sólo un poquito de pintura. Había color de rosa, azul y blanco, pero no lo suficiente para pintar de un solo color el cuarto.

—Tengo una idea—les dije a mis hermanitos—. Vamos a juntarlos todos—. Sergio y Héctor me ayudaron a vaciar de un bote a otro y observamos los colores mezclándose. Un nuevo color comenzó a aparecer, un poco morado pero más oscuro que el rosa. ¡Magenta!

Nos pusimos a pintar hasta que la pintura se nos terminó.

Mi mamá me enseñó cómo medir mi nueva pared magenta con un pedazo de estambre amarillo brillante que había quedado de la última cobijita que había tejido. Mi tío Pancho regresaba de nuevo a México y ahora yo podía quedarme con su cama, pero teníamos que decirle si la cama iba a caber.

Cortamos el pedazo de estambre del tamaño exacto de la cama. Corrimos todos hacia la casa de mi tío Pancho agitando el estambre en el aire y medimos su cama. ¡Perfecto! Ese pedacito de estambre amarillo era mágico.

Mamá showed me how to measure my new magenta wall with a piece of bright yellow yarn left over from the last baby blanket she had crocheted. Tío Pancho was going back to Mexico and said I could have his bed, but we had to let him know if it would fit.

We cut off the piece of yarn that showed us just how big the bed could be. We all ran to Tío Pancho's waving the piece of yarn. We measured his bed. Perfect! That yellow piece of yarn was magical.

A little later Tío Pancho arrived with my new bed tied to the roof of his car. I ran out and hugged him. Papá helped him carry the bed in and carefully ease it into place.

My brothers jumped up and down and everybody clapped. Then Raúl moved an empty wooden crate over to my new bed and stood it on end to make a bedside table.

"All you need now is a little lamp," my mother said.

Un poco más tarde mi tío Pancho llegó con mi nueva camita amarrada al techo de su coche. Corrí hacia afuera y lo abracé. Mi papá le ayudó a meter la cama y cuidadosamente la acomodó en su lugar.

Mis hermanos brincaron y brincaron y todos aplaudieron. Luego Raúl movió una caja de madera vacía y la acomodó a un lado de la camita para hacerla una mesita de noche.

—Lo único que ahora necesitas es una lamparita— dijo mi mamá.

Sacó una caja de zapatos repleta de estampillas *Blue Chip* que había coleccionado por años. Mi mamá y mi papá las recibían gratis cuando compraba comida o gasolina. Eran como pequeños premios que valían como dinero en tiendas especiales. Pero antes de poder usarlas, las teníamos que pegar en libritos para estampillas.

Así nos pusimos a lamber y a pegar estampillas sin parar. Cuando terminamos, mi papá nos llevó en el coche hasta la tienda de estampillas.

She brought out a shoe box stuffed with Blue Chip stamps she had been collecting for years. Mamá and Papá got them for free when they bought food or gas. They were like little prizes that could be used as money at special stores. But before we could spend them, we had to paste them into special stamp books.

We licked and licked and pasted and pasted. When we were done, Papá drove us to the stamp store.

$\mathcal{I}$ saw the lamp I wanted right away. It was as dainty as a beautiful ballerina, made of white ceramic glass with a shade that had ruffles around the top and bottom.

I shut my eyes. I was so excited yet so afraid we wouldn't have enough stamps to get it. Then I heard my mother's voice. "Yes, *mijita*. We have enough."

When we got home, I carefully set the new lamp on my bedside table. Then I lay on my new bed and stared at the ceiling, thinking. Something was still missing, the most important thing...

$\mathcal{E}$ nseguida que llegamos vi la lámpara que quería. Era tan delicada y bella como una bailarina, estaba hecha de cerámica de vidrio con una pantalla que tenía olancitos alrededor de la orilla de arriba a abajo.

Cerré los ojos. Estaba tan emocionada pero a la vez con miedo que no fuéramos a tener suficientes estampillas para conseguirla. Entonces oí la voz de mi mamá: —Sí, mijita. Tenemos suficientes.

Cuando llegamos a casa con mucho cuidado puse la nueva lámpara en mi mesita. Luego me recosté en mi nueva camita y miré hacia al cielo raso pensando. Todavía faltaba algo, lo más importante...

Books!

The next day I went to our public library and rushed home with my arms full of books, six to be exact. It was my lucky number because there were six children in my family.

¡Libros!

Al día siguiente fui a la biblioteca y me apuré para llegar a casa con los brazos llenos de libros. Eran exactamente seis. Ése era mi número de la suerte porque éramos seis niños en nuestra familia.

Esa noche prendí mi nueva lámpara y me puse a leer y leer. Mis dos hermanitos, Mario y Víctor se pararon en la puerta y abrieron las cortinas. Los invité a que entraran. Ellos se acurrucaron conmigo en mi nueva camita y les leí un cuento. Luego me dijeron: "Buenas noches" y regresaron a su cuarto.

That evening, I turned on my new lamp and read and read. My two littlest brothers, Mario and Víctor, stood in the doorway holding back the flour-sack curtain. I invited them in. They cuddled up on my new bed and I read them a story. Then we said goodnight and they went back to their room.

I felt like the luckiest, happiest little girl in the whole world. Everyone in our family had helped to make my wish come true. Before I could even turn out the light, I fell asleep peacefully under a blanket of books in my very own room.

Yo me sentí la niña más afortunada y feliz del mundo. Todos en mi familia me habían ayudado a realizar mi sueño. Antes de poder apagar la luz, me quedé dormida muy en paz bajo una cobija de libros en mi propio cuartito.

Amada Irma in 1958 with her five brothers around her, clockwise from bottom left: Mario, Héctor, Sergio, Raúl, and Víctor.

Amada Irma in 1960 with her parents, Consuelo and Sergio Hernández, and her brothers, clockwise from bottom center: Mario, Víctor, Sergio, Raúl, and Héctor.

Amada Irma in 1974 with her parents and her brothers, clockwise from bottom left: Mario, Víctor, Sergio, Raúl, and Héctor.

My Very Own Room is based on my own family story. My parents, like many of the parents of the children I now teach (and learn from), wanted to provide us with more space, but could not. However, they taught us strong values, supported our education, and insisted that we become bilingual. They wanted their children to be successful.

Today, most of us have been to college. Héctor and I have master's degrees in education and are elementary school teachers. Sergio is an engineer; Raúl is a supervisor in a California Youth Authority facility; Víctor is a housing sales agent; and Mario is a manager of a large grocery store. We are all committed to improving the lives of those who are struggling with the realities of poverty or adjusting to a new and different life.

—*Amada Irma Pérez*

For my mother and father, Arty, Marco, Nico, Michi, and my whole family including friends, teachers, students, colleagues, and all who have given me so much love, support, and encouragement. Also, Harriet, David, and Cindy. Mil gracias y mucho más... —A.I.P.

Always for you, Wendi / Siempre para ti, Wendi —M.C.G.

Amada Irma Pérez is a third-grade teacher in Oxnard, California, and a leading advocate of programs encouraging multicultural understanding. Like many of her students, Amada Irma was born in Mexico and came to the United States as a young child. *My Very Own Room* is based on her own family story. She lives with her family in Ventura, California.

Maya Christina Gonzalez is a painter and graphic artist. Her exquisite artwork has been praised by reviewers as "lively," "innovative," and "so bountiful it feels as if it's spilling off the pages." Maya is also a mentor artist in the Children's Book Press outreach program, LitLinks. She lives and plays in San Francisco, California.

Story copyright © 2000 by Amada Irma Pérez.
Illustrations copyright © 2000 by Maya Christina Gonzalez.

Publisher & Executive Director (current): Lorraine García-Nakata
Editors: Cynthia Ehrlich, Harriet Rohmer, David Schecter.
Spanish Language Editor: Francisco X. Alarcón
Spanish Translation: Consuelo Hernández
Design and Production: Cathleen O'Brien
Editorial and Production Assistant: Katherine Brown

Library of Congress Cataloging-in-Publication Data
Pérez, Amada Irma.
My very own room / story by Amada Irma Pérez; pictures by Maya Christina Gonzalez = Mi propio cuartito / escrito por Amada Irma Pérez; ilustrado por Maya Christina Gonzalez.
p. cm.
title: Mi propio cuartito.
Summary: With the help of her family, a resourceful Mexican American girl realizes her dream of having a space of her own to read and to think.
ISBN-13: 978-0-89239-223-0 (paperback)
[1. Bedrooms–Fiction. 2. Mexican Americans–Fiction. 3. Family life–Fiction. 4. Spanish language materials–Bilingual.] I. Title: Mi propio cuartito. II. Gonzalez, Maya Christina, ill. III. Title.
PZ3.P4655 2000 [E]–dc21 00-020769 CIP AC

Printed in Hong Kong by Marwin Productions
10 9 8 7 6 5 4 3 2 1

Distributed to the book trade by Publishers Group West

Children's Book Press is a nonprofit publisher of multicultural books for children. As a 501 (c)(3) nonprofit organization, our work is made possible in part by The AT&T Foundation, John Crew and Sheila Gadsden, The San Francisco Foundation, The San Francisco Arts Commission, Horizons Foundation, National Endowment for the Arts, Union Bank of California, CBP Board of Directors, and the Anonymous Fund of the Greater Houston Community Foundation. To contribute or to receive a catalog, visit **www.childrensbookpress.org** or write to Children's Book Press, 965 Mission Street, Suite 425, San Francisco, CA 94103. Quantity discounts available through the publisher for nonprofit use.